TOWN NOTICES:

The Cobtown Militia will muster in front of McGinty's Museum at 9:00 AM on the 4th. Wear your hatplates and yellow plumes!

— WARNING! —

Hans Van Ripper warns us that it might be dangerous to wear straw hats and bonnets around his goat "Buckeye." The animal is fond of dining on head-gear made of that material. ✶ ✶ ✶

THAT'S WHAT THEY SAY!

What your neighbors like best about the Fourth of July:

✶ We love to hear the sky go **BOOM!** We love to see the sky burst into colored stars!
–The Ravenell Twins

✶ I love the town parade. I can hardly wait until I am old enough to be a Volunteer and wear a yellow feather in my hat.
—Jasper Payne

✶ There's just as much good food on the 4th of July as at Thanksgiving! Not much beats eating a watermelon. I bet I could eat a whole one all by myself if I got the chance.
—Valentine McGinty

✶ There have been Van Rippers here in Cobtown long before there was a 4th of July! We started off being Dutch, then we were English. Now we are all Americans and I reckon that is the best of all! Things sure do change.
—Hans Van Ripper

✶ I love it that George Washington came over on the Mayflower so now we can be free!
—Rock Bub

Support the **COBTOWN SKYROCKETS,** our home town team!

HEDDY PEGGLER

OINKEY

LUCKY HART

CINNAMON HART

EDWIN HART

SKYROCKETS AND SNICKERDOODLES

A COBTOWN® STORY

From the Diaries of Lucky Hart

★

Written by

JULIA VAN NUTT

Illustrated by

ROBERT VAN NUTT

A Doubleday Book for Young Readers

APPLE JACK

JASPER PAYNE

VALENTINE

P.U.

BUCKEYE

ROCK BUB

For Edwin, who told us so much about Cobtown
J.V.N.

For my dad, who threw so many good pitches my way
R.V.N.

A DOUBLEDAY BOOK FOR YOUNG READERS
Published by Random House Children's Books
a division of Random House, Inc.
1540 Broadway
New York, New York 10036
Doubleday and the anchor with dolphin colophon are trademarks of
Random House, Inc.
Text copyright © 2001 by Julia Van Nutt
Illustrations copyright © 2001 by Robert Van Nutt

Cataloging-in-Publication Data is available from the Library of Congress.
ISBN: 0-385-32553-3

The text of this book is set in 15-point Greg.
Book design by Robert Van Nutt

Manufactured in the United States of America
June 2001
10 9 8 7 6 5 4 3 2 1

THE BIG GAME

"I don't feel so good, Grandma!" I said. "I feel sort of weak, like I might be catching something."

I was over at her house one summer day not too long ago.

"Come here and let's see." She held her hand up against my forehead. "I don't think you have a fever. Maybe you just need an excuse to go to bed. Are you worked up about tomorrow's baseball game?"

I nodded. "The Mugwumps are tough, Grandma," I whimpered.

"'It's not over till it's over'—you've heard that, haven't you?" Grandma asked. "It's a baseball saying, but it could pertain to any situation. It means that defeat is never a sure thing, even if that's the outcome you expect.

"Now, did you ever hear about my grandma Lucky Hart and the Fourth of July baseball game Cobtown played against the big city of Ploomajiggy? That happened way back in **1845**, one of the first years that baseball had an official rule book. It was quite a game!"

Grandma led the way up to the attic and rummaged through Lucky's old trunk. When she found the diary in question, we sat down for a good read.

Here's what we learned.

JULY 1, 1845

"We are going to see something great! The fireworks are here," Papa said.

Papa is excited about our Fourth of July celebration. And so am I. In a few days everybody in Cobtown will be dancing and singing after dark. It's the only time I am allowed to stay up all night. Last year I fell asleep, but I was only nine years old.

Fliberty was taking the fireworks off his wagon. Papa and I walked over to watch.

"Howdy, Mr. Hart." That's what Fliberty calls my papa. "I just heard some news about the Old County Map."

Fliberty went on to tell us about the huge old map stored at Ploomajiggy. It was made way back in the 1700s, and it shows every known town in this area. Last month, when they took the map from its box, they found that a mouse had eaten a hole in it. The part that once showed Cobtown had been swallowed by a critter. Now they are not even sure this _is_ Cobtown. We had a good laugh at that.

Oh my! Buckeye the goat is in the yard! I must run him off or he will eat the laundry hanging on the line! He will even eat the line! He will even eat the soap! And like it!

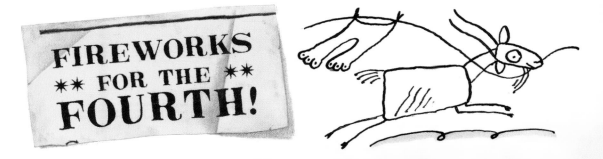

CARBUNCLE

JULY 2.

Here's what happened today. First, several men from the Cobtown & Ploomajiggy Rail-Road arrived in town. No amount of arguing from Virgil Squib, the station master, could stop them from nailing up a new sign. The sign says "Carbuncle"—their new name for Cobtown!

The men told Virgil that we have to show them our town marker if we want to be called Cobtown again. Imagine that!!!

No one has found the marker and no one can remember ever having seen it. Not even Old Hans, and he is our authority on local history.

I don't know what will come of it all.

This afternoon I met my good friend Jasper Payne at Apple Jack's orchard. Apple Jack is the trainer for our base ball team, the Cobtown Skyrockets. We will play a game against the Ploomajiggy Unbeatables at the Fourth of July celebration. Each team must have nine players. So far we only have eight. We need to find one more . . . and quickly!

"The art of the game comes in placing each player in the spot that most suits their natural abilities," Apple Jack told us. Then we heard a loud "Blam! Blam!"

"Jasper, I want you to play second base," Apple Jack said.

"Blam! Blam!"

"What is that racket?" Apple Jack looked towards the train station. "Blam! Blam!" We all walked over.

"Look, it's Rock Bub. His family lives so far off that we hardly ever see him in town," Jasper said.

And there he was, Rock Bub, in all his splendor, doing what he does best: throwing rocks. He was aiming at the new Carbuncle sign. "Blam!" He threw another rock and hit dead center of the big "C."

About that time Virgil stuck his head out of the ticket window. "Hey, you, Bub! I told you to stop. Like it or not, that Carbuncle sign is official rail-road property!" Virgil grabbed his broom and shook it.

"I've got an idea," Apple Jack whispered. "Bring Rock Bub over to my place. He'll make a fine pitcher for our team. That will give us the nine players we need."

"There's only one more thing," Jasper said. "Are we going to be the Cobtown Skyrockets or will we have to be the Carbuncle Skyrockets?"

Apple Jack's face turned pale. "Let's just wait and see," he said.

July 3

It felt bad to wake up in Carbuncle. I don't want to
be a Carbuncle Skyrocket. We were at Apple Jack's early
today to start our training.

Fliberty gave us new bats. He made them from ash
wood. He also made us some leather-covered balls.

Our base markers are sand-filled sacks that once
held Mule Pep. They were donated by Mr. Ravenell,
owner of the General Store.

Apple Jack had Rock Bub pitching old sorry apples to
us. Some exploded when we hit them. Buckeye the goat
gobbled up these "balls" after they landed.

My aunt Heddy Peggler stopped by with her little pig,
Oinkey. "There's a town meeting up at Ravenell's Store.
It's about this Carbuncle nonsense. Come on," she said.

We had to walk right past that Carbuncle sign to get
to Ravenell's. I couldn't help it. I started crying. I didn't
see a soul in town who was smiling.

I. B. Hootie, who prints the newspaper, was speaking
to the crowd. "As of yesterday, we all live in Carbuncle.
It's an ugly name and I don't know about you, but I
don't want to go around thinking that's where I'm from.
We must spread out and search for the old town marker
in the tall weeds and under any fallen trees."

Hans Van Ripper, whose family has been here from
Cobtown's earliest days, spoke up. "My family has long

prided itself on being the keepers of legend and lore. I looked in our trunk of old papers. I could find no mention of the town marker. I did, however, discover a lost recipe for snickerdoodles." He handed it to Aunt Heddy.

"Why, Hans! I remember snickerdoodles from when I was a little girl," Aunt Heddy said. "I'll bake up a special batch for the person who finds the Cobtown marker."

Then Mama spoke. "This is an important mission. We must not fail. Otherwise, folks will be calling us Carbunclians for the rest of our days."

So far, nobody has found it. I didn't get to taste a snickerdoodle. Now I have to go to sleep in Carbuncle again. Ugh!!!

Snickerdoodles

1 cup Lard or Butter	2 2/3 cups sifted Flour
1 cup Sugar	2 Tsp. Cream of Tartar
1 cup Molasses	1 Tsp. Corn Starch
2 Eggs	1 Tsp. Baking Soda
1 Tsp. Vanilla	1/2 Tsp. Salt

2 Tbsp. Sugar and 1 Tsp. Cinnamon set aside for Topping

Beat butter and sugar until light. Beat in molasses, eggs and vanilla. Sift together flour, cream of tartar, cornstarch, baking soda and salt. Add to mixture. Shape dough into 1" balls and roll in cinnamon-sugar mixture. Place 2" apart on an ungreased baking sheet. Bake in a hot oven for 8-10 minutes. Makes 6 dozen.

JULY 4, 1845

Boom! Boom! Boom! Boom!
They marched down the hill,
pounding the drum. Past
McGinty's Museum. Past Heddy
Peggler's back porch. Around
the bend at Payne's Tavern.
The Fourth of July festivities
started with a parade that
snaked through the town. Old
Hans led the marching. The flag

was flapping. Every member of the militia sported a
bright yellow plume. My heart was beating even faster
than Fliberty's drum, for today, my ball team was
playing against the Ploomajiggy Unbeatables.

Down at the Beaver Meadow I got a look at our
rivals. They were all laughing about being in Carbuncle
and boasting about how easily they were going to win.
Oh! That made me mad!

Our uniforms look like this:
Mama sewed us all yellow neck scarves
so we look like a team. I. B. Hootie made
our hats from folded newspaper.
"Carbuncle Skyrockets" was printed
on them. It reminded me that we had failed
to find the Cobtown marker.

The game started and Rock Bub threw balls that made those P.U.'s swing again and again . . . without ever making a hit. Only Valentine McGinty had a problem with this. As hind catcher, he was receiving the full force of these pitches and getting the air knocked out of him. Fliberty tied a partially full sack of Mule Pep around Valentine's neck to protect his stomach.

Then, "CRACK!" The P.U.'s' shortstop knocked one hard. It flew by me so fast that I didn't have a chance to catch it. That projectile even passed Sissy Dingle in the outfield. It kept going. The P.U.'s had hit a home run! The score was 1 to 0. Buckeye the goat reached the ball first and tried to swallow it, but it was too big. Meshack got it back, but Buckeye now had a wild glint in his eye.

Anybody who knows Buckeye understands that look. It means "I'm hungry and I'm gonna start eating anything I take a liking to." And that's more or less what happened next.

Buckeye eased up behind the umpire, who was squatting down low, and grabbed his straw hat. When the ump tried to grab it back, Buckeye ran off. And he's fast! Real fast!

He lit out towards the train station. Jasper scooted after him. Then, just before Jasper could reach the hat, Buckeye climbed straight up the ivy that grows next to the station. In a flash that goat was up on the station roof, waving the hat around and looking real proud. Then he took a big bite out of it.

None of us had ever seen a goat walk straight up a vine before.

Valentine pulled the ivy leaves back and peered underneath. All of a sudden, he let out with a whoop. "Come look at this!" he shouted.

He tore away at the vines that had grown round and round a big stone post. We saw words cut into the stone:

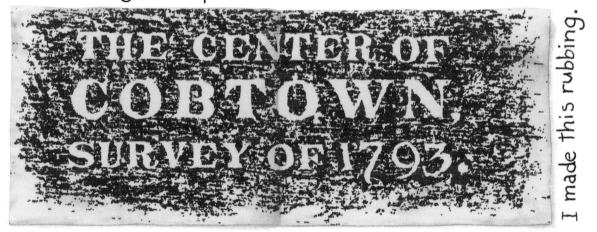

THE CENTER OF COBTOWN, SURVEY OF 1793.

I made this rubbing.

We had found the lost marker! Everybody laughed when Jasper cried out, "Hoo-ray! We ain't in Carbuncle anymore!"

We were ready to be the COBTOWN SKYROCKETS again! I. B. Hootie brought us new hats. A fighting spirit was kindled in our hearts. Now we had to win,

for COBTOWN!

I hit one hard enough to get on first base. Jasper was next at bat and he was full of fire. He hit the ball so far that no one could catch it. I crossed home base to tie the game.

Jasper ran from first to second base and then to third. He was hollering "Cobtown! Cobtown!" As he rounded third, the P.U. baseman stuck his foot out and made Jasper fall. Jasper twisted his ankle so badly that he had to leave the game.

We still needed a runner to come across home to score. But who could it be? The rules said you had to be under 13 years old to play. There was no one else in town that age!

Then Apple Jack had an idea. "We need a runner and I know who it will be. The rule book doesn't say a player has to be human! Jasper, I'll need your yellow scarf."

Lucky Hart

RULES & REGULATIONS
OF THE
Recently invented Game
OF
BASE BALL

AS ADOPTED BY
the
Ploomajiggy
Base Ball Association
1845

He walked over to Oinkey and tied it around his neck.

"A substitute runner will step in for Jasper Payne," Apple Jack announced. The crowd cheered as Aunt Heddy led her little pig over to third base.

After some arguing, the umpire agreed to let Oinkey play but said he had to tag home plate to score a run.

Now Meshack came to bat. All he had to do was knock the ball far enough to get Oinkey home. Then we would win the game. Some of us were wondering if Oinkey could do it.

"CRACK!" Meshack's bat swatted the ball high . . . past everybody, and he started running. At third base Oinkey watched the ball. It hadn't occurred to him to run to home base. But Aunt Heddy, who was near home plate, threw her head back and gave one of her pig yodels. That always makes him run to her. And so Oinkey took off.

"Run, Oinkey! Run!" we yelled. Meanwhile, one of the P.U.'s grabbed the ball and threw it right at Oinkey. It would have hit the little pig, except Oinkey veered away. But now he was confused. He stopped and watched all the P.U.'s scrambling after the ball.

"Run, Oinkey!" we screamed. But Oinkey didn't seem to understand.

That's when Aunt Heddy reached into her apron pocket. She took something out and tossed it onto home plate. It was a snickerdoodle! Oinkey understood that! He ran like the wind and tagged the base with his snout. We had scored the winning run!

The Cobtown Skyrockets had beaten the Ploomajiggy Unbeatables!

Now I'm back home. Mama thinks I'm up here in my room resting, but I'm just too excited. I am ready to dance and eat and sing and watch the sky light up with exploding fireworks.

This is sure to be a Fourth of July to remember!

July 5

This Fourth of July has been the best one ever. We had good music all through the night. Jerico Dingle played the fiddle and Apple Jack joined in on his cider jug. Jasper played the spoons. I grabbed Sissy Dingle's hand and started dancing.

We had so much food. Payne's Tavern provided sweet potato biscuits and Brunswick stew. Rock Bub's family brought turtle soup. Aunt Heddy contributed jars of her watermelon rind pickles.

She also surprised us with snickerdoodles. They are sweet and full of cinnamon. Old Hans proclaimed them the official Cobtown Cookie.

I. B. Hootie made a speech. "This day we have celebrated the founding of our great country. We have regained our rightful name, Cobtown. We have defeated a rival, the Ploomajiggy Unbeatables. But let us not forget tonight that no matter if we are from Cobtown or Ploomajiggy, we celebrate this day as Americans."

Come join us and CELEBRATE the 4th of July with FIREWORKS!

GEORGE WASHINGTON

We heard a "Dong! Dong!" Fliberty was ringing the town bell.

Then Professor McGinty, Valentine's papa, addressed the town. "Today, my fellow Americans, we celebrate this great land, but let us not forget the miracle we witnessed. The actions of a small member of our community found our lost marker. I refer to Buckeye. In his honor, I have arranged a stage production of BUCKEYE, THE GOAT THAT SAVED COBTOWN at McGinty's Museum and Olio of Oddities. We shall re-enact this marvelous discovery every Fourth of July from here on, lest we forget the magnificent antics of this astonishing animal. Refreshments will be available."

Mama addressed the crowd next. "Listen, everybody. Lucky's father and Fliberty are preparing the fireworks. Edwin asked me to remind you that there will be <u>two</u> displays of fireworks, one very soon and the other at the end of the party. That means tomorrow morning at first light. Now, to get us in the spirit, let's all sing 'Yankee Doodle.'"

Everybody started clapping their hands and stamping their feet. Jerico Dingle struck up the fiddle. And we sang with all our hearts.

Then the night lit up in bursts of sparkling light. Boom! The sky exploded and we cheered. We had more dancing and more eating. The Ravenell twins fell asleep on a blanket. But I didn't, not this year.

Just before sunrise, Papa asked us to face our flag and sing the "Oh say" song. The words to this song are all about the War of 1812. Old Hans fought in that war so we could keep our independence. The song describes the blasts of light from the guns and cannons.

Valentine's mother led the singing as Papa started another round of fireworks. As the sky took on the first dim glow of the new day, we looked at our flag and sang. "Oh, say, can you see by the dawn's early light, what so proudly we hailed at the twilight's last gleaming?" And we could. We could still see our flag. "And the rockets' red glare! The bombs bursting in air!" It was really happening. Yes, our star-spangled banner <u>still</u> proudly waves over this land of the free.

＊ Lucky Hart ＊

Cobtown, 1845

THE COBTOWN 🦉 OBSERVER

I.B. HOOTIE: CHIEF CORRESPONDENT, EDITOR, PRINTER AND PUBLISHER.

FIREWORKS ** FOR THE ** FOURTH!

GET READY for the biggest and best 4th of July ever! Things will start at 10 AM. Drums will beat, fifes will tweet and flags will wave as the Volunteers of the Cobtown Militia lead the traditional **GRAND PARADE** through town. It will end in the Beaver Meadow where our Cobtown Skyrockets will play against the Ploomajiggy Unbeatables in a game of * **BASE BALL!** * This is sure to be an exciting match. Apple Jack Peggler, trainer of the young Skyrockets, tells us that our home team has honed its skills, studied the rules, and is ready to try its hand at this new sport. May the best team win-- and we will!!! * *

Liberty 1776 1845.

Looks like kitchens all over town are mighty busy these days getting things ready for the annual * **BIG PICNIC!** * I know there are quite a few of us bachelors looking forward to all the good eating we will be doing! All that fine food will give us strength for the **MUSIC & DANCING** that will follow. I am sure Jerico Dingle is tuning up his fiddle right now! No doubt the high point of the celebrations will be Mr. Edwin Hart's all-night extravaganza of **FIREWORKS!**

COBTOWN VANISHES!

WELL, NOT REALLY, but it seems that we have somehow disappeared from the Official County Survey Map kept in the Ploomajiggy Hall of Records. It looks like some critter showed its good taste by eating that portion of the map that contained Cobtown! Although we are still here, they say there is no official record of our town name or location as established by the survey of 1793. There is no telling what mischief the scheming political scoundrels over at the County Seat will make of this. We will just have to wait and see. *

FINE WEATHER is predicted for the 4th of July. Hoo-Ray!